I0628721

# G'Dog

*short stories by*

## Sarah Leamy

*Finishing Line Press*
Georgetown, Kentucky

# G'Dog

OTHER BOOKS include:

*When No One's Looking* (2010)
*Lucky Shot* (2012)
*Lucky Find* (2014)
*Van Life* (2016)
*Before Coffee* (2017)
*Before Kibble* (2018)
*Hidden* (2021)

Publisher: Leah Huete de Maines
Editor: Christen Kincaid
Cover Art: Sarah Leamy
Author Photo: Sarah Leamy
Cover Design: Elizabeth Maines McCleavy


Order online: www.finishinglinepress.com
also available on amazon.com

Author inquiries and mail orders:
Finishing Line Press
PO Box 1626
Georgetown, Kentucky 40324
USA

# Eva March Tappan

Eva March Tappan was born on 26th December 1854 in Blackstone, Massachusetts, America. She is well known as a factual as well as fictional writer, but spent her early career as a teacher. Tappan was the only child of Reverend Edmund March Tappan and Lucretia Logée, and received her education at the esteemed Vassar College. This was a private coeducational liberal arts college, in the town of Poughkeepsie, New York, from which she graduated in 1875. Here, Tappan was a member of Phi Beta Kappa, the oldest honour society for the liberal arts and sciences, widely considered as the nations most prestigious society. She also edited the *Vassar Miscellany,* a college publication.

After leaving her early education, Tappan began teaching at Wheaton College, one of the oldest institutions of higher education for women in the United States, founded in 1834 and based in Norton, Massachusetts. She taught Latin and German here, from 1875 until 1880, before moving on to the Raymond Academy in Camden, New Jersey where she was associate Principal until 1894. Tappan also received a graduate degree in English Literature from the University of Pennsylvania. This allowed her to pursue her first love, that of reading and writing, and she taught as head of the English department at the English High School at Worcester, Massachusetts.

It was only after this date that Tappan began her literary career, writing about famous characters in history, often aimed at educating children in important historical themes and epochs. Some of her better known works include, *In the Days of William the Conqueror* (1901) and *In the Days of Queen Elizabeth* (1902), *The Out-of-Door Book* (1907), *When Knights Were Bold* (1911) and *The Little Book of the Flag* (1917). Tappan never married, being a happy singleton, and died on 29th January 1930, aged seventy-five.

# Table of Contents

*This one is for
Harold the Handsome*

## Sheeplifting

—Go on, Harold. Go pee. The writer opened the door and checked the street for traffic. It was quiet.—Go on, I trust you.

Harold was an old dog, well, not exactly old, just the far side of middle-aged. He was a good dog, honest and reliable. The writer wandered back inside, sat at the desk and stared at that metal bland object she loved more than him. He was bored. He decided to go get himself a treat.

Harold walked down the hill to Main Street. When the voice at the corner said Wait, he waited. When the beeps began and all the humans walked, Harold walked. He walked past the temptation of the popcorn maker, the bagel maker, and trotted past the booze seller and into Shaw's, the grocery store. He'd never been inside before. It was all rather exciting. The doors opened when he stood there. The cashiers smiled at him. The other humans petted him. He was a big boy, with thick black fur and a red bandana. He looked pretty good and he knew it. His tail wagged, sweeping from side to side, and so he strolled past the carrots and spinach and towards the butchers in the back. He sniffed and found heaven.

Rows and rows of dead animals. No hunting needed.

He stood there, did Harold, nose sniffing deeply, jowls dribbling, and tail picking up speed. He stood on his hind legs and peered into the fridges. Sheep. Cow. Pig. Chicken.

Which should he pick? Sheep, he decided. You don't come across them often, not something he gets to chase for himself. He chose a decently sized lamb chop with bone and clamped his teeth into it and drooled. He lay down for a quick chew.

Yes, it was good. He took it with him as he strolled back down aisle three, wondering why the writer always made him wait outside. He had just stepped through the magically opening doors when a voice stopped him.

—Wait!

Harold is a good boy. He waited.

—What do you think you're doing?

A hand clamped onto his collar and in surprise Harold yelped. He dropped the meat. The hand let go to pick it up.

—I'll have to call your owner. Where are your tags, dog? Don't you have any? Should I call Animal Control to take you? Come here, dog. Poor thing, don't you have a home?

Home? Harold thought of home. He bared his yellowing teeth and then ran. Oh boy, did Harold run. Up Main Street, along State Street, waiting at the crossing like a good boy and then home up the stairs to his home.

His writer hadn't moved. She glanced up at him standing in the doorway.

—Did you go pee?

Harold turned around. He'd forgotten about that. He walked back downstairs and thought about getting a treat.

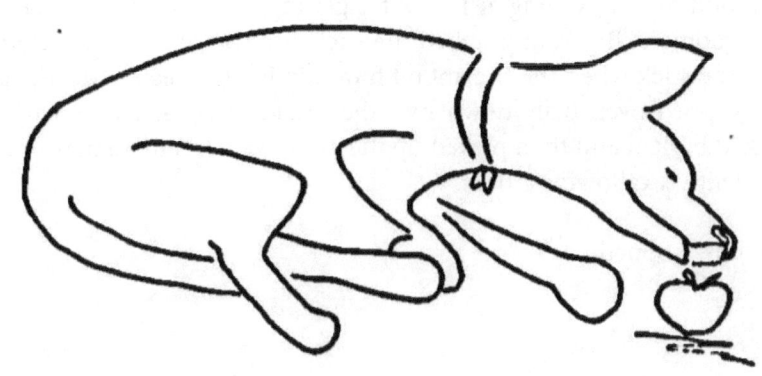

## Sticks

There was once an ant called Adam. Adam was walking home after a long day following orders when it began to rain. The normally arid arroyo filled and a whoosh of water flung little Adam sideways into the middle of Lake Puddle. Adam paddled. A dog watched from within this mud bowl, holding a stick in his mouth. Derek the dog loved water, he loved to roll and dive and splash and swim but it didn't look like that was true for little Adam Ant who was desperately trying to do the butterfly across the pond. Derek dropped his stick, not so much out of pity but rather because he forgot it was in his mouth. Adam Ant crawled up onto it just as a Big Foot came storming up, all wellies and loud mouth, yelling at Derek for getting so dirty after the day at the groomers. Big Foot grabbed the stick and was about to hit Derek with the stick when the fire ant bit him. Big Foot squealed in surprise and slipped over, belly down into the muddy waters. Derek barked barked barked and then picked up the stick again, ready to play fetch, accidently swallowing Adam.

The rain stopped.

**Sharing is Caring**

Rosie ate roadkill soup for dinner.

The aroma filled the apartment and the downstairs neighbor thumped her roof when the smoke alarm screamed overhead.

Should I give her some? I asked but Rosie shook her head. It was all hers.

The goose gizzards and squashed squirrel combo wasn't one I'd have thought of but Rosie claimed it was a traditional dish in these parts. These Vermonters like to add cheese—grated Cabot cheddar—to the dish once it's cooled down for 36 seconds. Rosie is very precise about us fitting in.

We don't.

Stephen asked for a glass of milk instead. Harold wanted the squirrel tail to clean his teeth with. I ate the cheese. Rosie cleaned her bowl. The snow fell.

It's all go on a Friday night in Montpelier.

In the middle of the night, Rosie woke me. She had a tummy ache. We went outside for some fresh air but it didn't quite work out like that. Rosie ran down the stairs and threw up. Outside the neighbor's bedroom window, she heaved and retched and splattered the soup bile across fresh snow. Finally Rosie came back to bed, feet heavy on the wooden steps. The neighbor thumped her ceiling once again.

I put the last of the soup in a container and left it on the downstair's doorstep. With a note saying, Enjoy.

## Be Mindful of Where You Place Your Photographs

There was once a poor writer who had two little dogs. The youngest was sent to the corner of Main and State every day to gather the news. Once when she waited a long time before hearing any, a beautiful monkey appeared who told the little dog a story about an elephant with a red tusk. Then in a twinkling he vanished. The little dog told the writer, but the writer wouldn't believe the dog. Then one day the dog brought home a photograph of the red-tusked elephant and told the writer that the beautiful monkey had given it to her and that he'd said he would come for her when the tusk faded to pink. The writer put the photograph on the windowsill. One morning, the little dog didn't show up for breakfast. The writer went and found the dog dead, but looking adorable with her tongue sticking out. The photograph had faded that same morning. The tusk was pink.

## Throw in a Clean Blanket

A nasal voice barked out her questions.

The Texan syntax of an educated and older female carried down the hallway. Her tutting and sheeshing and click-clacking on the linoleum slowly worked its way closer. I didn't move. What was the point? It was Saturday, the Santa Fe Human Shelter comes alive on Saturdays; it's a nice thing to do after a walk in the park, right? Adopt a friendly human as a pet? Someone like me?

My room was small, pale green, and the bed was lumpy. I curled up, staring at the blank walls. Boy, it stank in here. Not me, mind, no, I'm usually quite clean but to be honest my tum had been a bit wobbly since I got here, what was that, a week ago? Oh, time drags when you're having fun.

Not.

—Oh, will you look at that one. What's his story?

The footsteps of the supposedly friendly attendant shuffled closer to the stall. He turned on the overhead fluorescents to wake me. It was nowhere near dinnertime, not that I was hungry, the food there left a lot to be desired. My back was turned for a reason. I ignored them both.

—Her last owner died, the attendant explained, mouth full yet again.— Then another family had her for a while, but the mother said that Queenie was too grumpy. Or too old, she didn't want kids climbing all over her. Not a maternal bone in that skinny body.

—It's female?

—Yes, I know, you can't tell but a good bath would be all it took. I'd even throw in a clean blanket and some meds for the diarrhea.

—Well, let's have a look, shall we?

The door opened and finally I peeked over my left shoulder.

A small Boston terrier, no bows in her collar, fur trimmed, short nails, and holding a short leash walked in—well, that explained the accent. She was much too tidy, too pretty, and too bleeding small for someone like me, so I turned back to the comfort of cold concrete. She click-clacked closer to me. Nice smell, a mix of wet dog, bone breath, and grass, well, all I'm saying is that she smelled nice. Good enough for me. I sat up on the edge of the bedframe. She held up a paw to me. I high-fived her. Dogs like it when you do that: Turn tricks. I know how to play the game; I'd do anything to get out of there.

—Does she understand us, do you think? Do you know her breeding?

—Well, she's English—in theory—but she seems smart enough for farming stock, look at those hands! All scars and sunspots, she's no lady.

The Bostonian pet me awkwardly; dogs really don't know how. She scooted her bum across my blanket, apparently unperturbed by my gurgling belly and bad breath. I'd love to brush my teeth again. And wash my blanket.

She sniffed my teddy bear's bum, shaking her head. My hands were clenched. If she licks Timmy, I'll fucking kill her.

She didn't. She left him laying on my lap. I shoved Timmy under my tee shirt, out of reach, and watched her with eyes a steely grey. I blinked first.

With a deep sigh, she barked,—Sheesh, it's such a shame when we get rid of humans because they're too old. She's only fifty, you say? If only I'd live to that age, poor thing.

The chubby attendant in his Lab coat smirked,—you already have, haven't you? No offence like, but little dogs like you live a long time. And you sure are little. The question is, will you be able to manage a brute like this one? She's not so house-trained, you know, terrible in the city, can't walk on a leash to save her life, and at the kitchen table? No manners. A right blue collar one she is.

—It's fine. I live in the country. She can have the run of the place. Right, Queenie? You want to come live in the mountains? Hundreds of acres to explore and a room of your own? You can even bring your teddy bear. I'd just like a little company around the place, not much though. Don't be needy, alright Queenie? Or I'll bring you back.

I'd listened carefully and shook her paw again, thinking, anything is better than this.

The attendant threw me a look,—I'll be glad to see the back of her. Messy bugger.

—I'll take her, said my new protector. How much?

—For her? Free. And good riddance. Take the bloody woman, will you? We need the space for a cute toddler.

—Oh. You have toddlers? Any girls? Potential breeders?

The attendant nodded.—A few.

I must have whimpered as the Terrier patted me on the head awkwardly, messing up my hair, and saying,—I'll be back. Honest.

The attendant shut the door with a wink. The corridor went quiet. I lay back down and faced the concrete wall. I wanted a home of my own. My tummy rumbled.

## Saved by a Mouse Called Mikaela

One day when Cat Stephen was napping, an annoying mouse called Mikaela began skipping up and down him. Cat Stephen woke up in a bad mood. He placed his paw upon Mikaela and with a terrifically wide yawn, opened his mouth to eat the mouse.

—Sorry, sorry! cried Mikaela, let me free! I'm not worth it, all skin and bones. Save me, oh save me! I'll do the same for you some day.

Tickled pink at the idea, Stephen let the mouse run away, and chuckled as he dozed.
Only a few days later, Cat Stephen fell into a trap set for a Heffalump. The net caught him unawares. The little mouse happened to walk past as Cat Stephen was hung up. She squealed in delight. Mikaela climbed up the tree and began to gnaw at the ropes. Stephen watched. It took a while. He tried not to complain about the motion sickness. Three hours and ten minutes later, the mouse let out a triumphant squeak. The net fell to the ground as did Cat Stephen.

He was hungry though.

## The Quack

Once upon a time, Daisy the Duck lived with Dribbles the Dog. They didn't always get along. Daisy thought that Dribbles was a bit of a dick. She always criticized her friend. Her comments were to help Dribbles become less sniffy with those different to himself, or so said Daisy.

Daisy the Duck had spent years next door to a library which had inflated her sense of self. She thought of herself as a psychologist. She informed all the neighbors that Dribbles the Dog was so much nicer these days now that he was in listen-therapy. She also mentioned how she could cure others—for a fee—naturally. She was a quack doctor.

One day, a long day, Dribbles looked Daisy over very carefully.

—My friend, he said,—I've been told, by yourself, repeatedly, that you cure anything and everyone. But have you taken a close look at yourself recently? Have you tried your own medicine? Tastey? No? Otherwise, I should advise you to keep your opinions to yourself. Oh, and I'm handing you your notice. You have to move out by Friday. Good luck, duck.

## A Great Plan

The dogs called a meeting to decide on how to free themselves from the tyranny of the terrible tiger. They hardly dared move off their beds for fear of this tiger, which really was only a ten pound cat called Stephen. Stephen attacked ankles, bit tails, hung off collars, ate their food right out from under the dogs noses, and dared the two dogs to do something about it.

They didn't.

Many plans were discussed but Harold didn't think much of them. Rosie was a great one for wild ideas. Harold shook his head. At last Rosie said:

I have a plan. It is very simple. I know it will succeed. All we have to do is build a wall around the tiger. When it is built, he won't be able to come into our comfortable world. He will have to fend for himself and get his own food. Our tails will be safe.

The two dogs thought long and hard. It seemed a good plan. Who can scale a wall? They wouldn't be able to, that's for sure. The dogs were surprised they'd not thought of such an easy plan before.

The two dogs built such a wall while the cat napped. They used bedding from the bedroom, pillows, cushions, coats and boots. It was a very good wall, a solid wall, a huge wall. The dogs lay down and fell asleep assured that they were finally safe from the tiger-like cat. Stephen woke up, glanced at the bedding, and hopped over. He let the sleeping dogs lie and ate their kibble. It needed some cream.

## Missing

There was once an oldish writer who lived in a forest. The woods were full of shadows and creepy crawlies. The woman wrote every morning. In the afternoons she took her pet snake and a turtle for a short walk in the vegetable patch. Evenings she wrote more. It was a good life. The only problem was that she thought her work sucked. No one wanted to read it. She had no agent, no editor, and no publisher. It's true: Her stories were boring. Nothing much happened in them. The characters were flat. The dialogue was more like a monologue.

One day, she walked around the cauliflowers in her garden with her pets and she gave herself a choice. Either she had to throw away all that she had done, the novels and novellas, the prose poems, essays and short stories, and of course those ridiculous fables with no knot of meaning. Or she had to sit down and revise the lot of it.

She hated revision.

She pondered and paused as she wandered and wondered. A sudden storm sent her back to her cabin; the snow and ice, rain and sleet drove her inside. She opened the woodstove to feed it, that is after taking out Mickey, her pet monkey, and his stuffed toy. She threw in her papers. All of them. Six crates worth of words. It was a raucous fire. The snake was drawn to the heat. The old woman placed him on top of the stove for warmth. The turtle was lost outside in a food coma. The monkey climbed around the writer's neck and shoulders with a pencil in hand and his toy in the other. Mickey ate the pencil tip.

When the storm died out so did the fire. The forest calmed down and so did the old writer. Her angst had burned up with the ashes. She went for a walk wearing the furry scarf called Mickey, saying, you're not my monkey, but she petted him anyway.

A literary agent from New York City drove up to the cabin in a rental car. She had read about how much of hermit this newly discovered writer was and she came prepared with a contract. The agent knocked on the thick wooden door. It swung open. The home was empty yet tidy. There was a lingering heavy aroma of roast chicken. The agent snuck around, and upon seeing no laptop, pencils, nor even any notebooks, she threw the contract onto the warm embers in the woodstove. She drove away through the writer's ruts.

The turtle woke up alone. Hungry.

## Big Bump Day

—Don't worry about me. The nurse will take good care of me, honest. Go on, Mum, Rosie's waiting for you in the truck. I'll see you later.

Harold let himself be weighed as I watched, hovering. My chin wobbled. He stared at me, both of us stoic as the nurses and doctors talked over us.

That C-word.

The one no one wants to hear was whispered behind my back and my stomach clenched as I fake-smiled at my boy, thinking, Let's keep calling it a lump, that's all, a lump, a bump.

—Big Bump Day, right, Harry? I joked and he smiled slightly, a turn of lips, a glimpse of white teeth and that flash of red, the lump, the bump, the one pushing his teeth, shifting his jaw, pushing through his bones and I swallowed again, a taste of acid rain scarred my gut.

—I'll be fine, he reminded me.

I hugged him and stood back so the nurse could take him away from me.

Nodding at the receptionist, I walked back outside to my truck. Rosie waited in the front seat, soaking up the sunshine. Oblivious as only a younger sibling could be.

I looked back at the animal hospital, bent over, threw up.

## Be Careful of What You Do for Others

There was once a stay-at-home travel blogger who had two pet goats. She took care of those goats rather well, spoiling them with the best organic food, regular baths, and walks in the park. She talked to them constantly. One day she sent the oldest out to get her a treat from the farmer's market on State Street. He ran down the hill. He ran past the market and straight onto Rt. 2. He ran up Vermont and across Hero Islands into New York. He ran past the tourists in their RVs along Lake Erie. He ran past cows in Wisconsin, cowboys in Nebraska, moose in Montana and even increased his speed over the mountains into Washington. The grizzlies didn't have a chance. The old goat was tired by the time he stuck his hooves in the Pacific. He knew what she'd wanted back home in her apartment on Ocean View Estates. He ran home all the way back along Rt. 2. He was fit, lean, a marathon machine. He ran up to the travel blogger and told her all about his trip. She took notes. She then asked if he'd brought her a treat because he'd been gone rather a long time and it wasn't on, no, it really was quite inconvenient. The goat choked on her words and hawked up her treat from deep within his second stomach. It landed at her feet. The pet goat keeled over then and there, dead as a Sunday roast. The travel blogger wiped off the bile from the rock at her feet and licked it. Salt, she said, sea salt, that'll be useful later.

## Work Ethics

Adam is a fire ant.

He works very hard even in summer when it finally stops snowing and sometimes it doesn't rain. On Main Street at the bridge over a small river, Graham the grasshopper was bouncing around working on his suntan. Adam struggled past, heaving a cumbersome weed on his way back to the family's storeroom. It was always the same, those insects are so darn lazy but not Adam oh not Adam dammit.

—Why not stop and chat a while, asked the grasshopper scratching his soft underbelly, -instead of breaking a sweat?

—I am doing my duty. I am following orders. I am part of the greater good. And, I am a lean mean working machine.

—Who cares about any of that? said Graham with a grin.—It's a beautiful day in the neighborhood and pub is open. Care for a drink? My treat?

Adam shook his tiny head and went back to work, muttering about free-loaders. They saw each other there every afternoon at three. They did not talk to each other. Graham grew fat and happy, he tanned up nicely too, all crispy and crunchy.

When the weather turned back to winter, Graham was on the bridge again, waiting for the pub to open. Adam did not show up. He was home having a decent meal in comfort. However, Graham was alone in the snow and growing skinnier by the day. Poor Graham. The pub was closed for the season.

## A Dog's Dinner

One Sunday afternoon, an Indoor Dog visited a friend who lived outside in a run down shack without running water or heat. They had a bit of a crush on each other. For lunch, the Outdoor Dog served old bones with a side of fresh dung, an old chicken carcass, and a bucket of dirty puddle water for their beverages. The Indoor Dog ate very lightly, claiming she was watching her figure, nibbling a little of this and a licking of that and by her manner making it plain that she was only being polite.

After the meal the friends had a long chat, or rather the Indoor Dog talked about her life inside. The Outdoor Dog listened. They then went to bed under the porch in the sand and cobwebs, it was all very innocent and there was no hanky-panky even though the Outdoor Dog got a good sniffing in. In his sleep the Outdoor Dog dreamed he was an Indoor Dog with all the luxuries and delights of such a life. The next day when the Indoor Dog asked the Outdoor Dog to go home with her, the Outdoor Dog said yes and got an immediate boner.

This could be his lucky day.

When they reached the apartment in which the Indoor Dog lived, they crept past the gatekeeper at the elevator and took to the stairs, paws padding softly up the carpet. They found in the kitchen a counter full with Sunday dinner, gravy, roast chicken with crisp crunchy skin, mashed potatoes, some green stuff that neither of them wished for, and pie with cream.

The Outdoor Dog had not seen such a spread before.

Just as he jumped up on the counter and began to tear his way through the plated meal, footsteps approached the kitchen. The Indoor Dog peed herself. She hid under the table, ears flat and tail tucked out of sight.

The Outdoor Dog was on his own.

He flew off the table, mouth full of flesh, and pushed his way past the yelling humans in the hallway, tail high, ears flapping in delight.

On his way out the apartment, the Outdoor Dog barked at his former crush,—I'll admit this was fun, I'd do it again. Let me know when.

He raced back to his shack, grabbed an old bone, and fell asleep with it in his mouth. He was tired.

## Hot Tempers and Cool Water

One April Tuesday, a pale white Wolf was lapping at a rushing river, full of fresh blue snowmelt. When looking up, the Wolf noticed a scrawny brown Coyote on the other side of the Rio Grande. He put down his chicken sandwich on a near by rock and stared. The Coyote was also enjoying a cool fresh beverage on that unseasonably warm afternoon.

The Wolf called out,—how dare you drink from my river? You will dirty it.

—It's the warm weather if you ask me that is causing the flooding of this river, reaching us both. We all share in the bounty of this world. Let's go skinny-dipping. Want to? I'm game.

The Wolf was not having it, he'd been having a bad week, his popularity in the pack was waning and he needed to blame someone as obviously it was not his fault and never would be his fault.

—It's my snow. It's my mountain. It's my river! The Wolf shouted, waving his tiny pale paws in the air in frustration.—You shall not drink from my river or ...!

The Coyote took a dive into the river with a splash. He washed himself thoroughly if quickly.—Oh really, said the Coyote, as cool as a snowflake landing on an ice-cream cone, or so he wished.—What are you going to do about it? It's not like you could do much with those hamster paws of yours.

—I'll fucking kill you, you damn foreigner, stealing from me and mine.

The Wolf rushed into the raging river but before he could cross to the coyote, a chunk from that killer glacier clunked him good and proper and knocked him out cold onto the north bank of the Rio Grande. The Wolf drowned.

The Coyote hopped across the great divide. He had a look around, thought of his family, and headed back home. He had a quick swim first though. The water was nice and cooling for hot tempers.

## Where Do All Our Teeth Go?
*(Science Class, Mr. Finch)*

Last week when I turned nine, I determined that it was time I found out what happens to all the lost teeth.

I set out one September afternoon with all the required equipment to discover their fate. Madison, Wisconsin, was having a warm yet damp spell and the trees were heavy with wet leaves. It had been a long summer, and I liked being outside and busy. I hiked along East Williamson Street with a happy gait, excited to have a mission that afternoon.

I picked a boy of seven or thereabouts to follow. He has a twin sister, and since both had gaps in their front teeth, they were a good bet that soon enough the tooth fairy would be visiting their abode once again. Outside their home was a wonderful willow tree that became my temporary fort. I settled in. My dad's monocular dangled from a shoestring around my skinny neck. I must have dozed off as I almost missed the flashy tooth fairy in her sequins and a pair of wellies as she flew by on her way to room #3 upstairs, left, and with the door slightly propped open—not that I know Mike's place, or at least not this week since he wouldn't talk to me after the food fight at school when I got him in the neck with a brussel sprout. Well, anyway, by the time that tooth-snatcher returned I was prepared to chase her down. The jar of peanut butter was back in my daypack. I pounded the pavement, chasing the tooth fairy skipping ahead with Mike's front tooth in a baggy.

Finally the pursuit terminated at a warehouse on the edge of town by the bowling alley. I propped my backpack against an oak tree—I recognized the leaf pattern from Mr. Finch's class.

The brick building was an abandoned cheese-packing factory. Is this why dairy is good for our teeth?

It was a long and tedious evening wait, all forty-seven minutes dragged. When the tooth fairy returned to continue her scavenging for wobbly teeth, she was not alone. In fact, a whole short-bus full of fairies rumbled past my hiding spot. Once they were out of sight, I snuck through the gate and crawled up close, commando style, to see exactly what they did with the dental detritus. Not much. All I noted through the murky glass was this, a step van, two dog beds, and a fort made of cardboard boxes. Suddenly the engine grumbled to life, and I fell off my milk crate. Just as I was brushing off the mud from my knee socks, the step van trundled past. A chihuahua and a terrier sat up front, each one wore a lovely white necklace of teeth.

On the side of the van was a hand-painted sign: Ankle Biters Accessories.

Now I know. I walked home to write up my findings.


P.S. Dad, when I handed in this report to Mr. Finch, he said it was 'very imaginative if unrealistic.' It's because he has a chihuahua named Tristan, who I hate by the way. That horrid dog knocked that tooth out of me last week when we were playing in the school yard. That's why I didn't get a good grade, honest Dad. Mr. Finch hates me. So does his stupid dog.

P.P.S. Can the tooth fairy pay me for that tooth now?

## Be Mindful of Who Buys You Beer

There once was a poor writer who had two friends. The oldest was sent to town every day to gather funds. Once when she had gone a long way before finding any cans to redeem, a beautiful meterman appeared who helped her buy a six-pack and carried it home for her. Then with a shuddering twinkle and a tinkle, he vanished. The friend told the writer, but the writer couldn't or wouldn't believe her. Then one day the friend brought home another full six-pack and said the meter-man had given it to her and he'd said he would come back again when the cans were empty. The writer put the six-pack in the fridge. One morning the friend didn't get out of bed. The writer went and found her friend passed out in her rumpled knickers but looking lovely. The cans in the fridge were empty that same morning.

Sarah Leamy is an award-winning author of various novels, short stories, travel memoirs, and cartoons. She is a multimedia artist, known for combining storytelling with images. Her work can be found on *Los Angeles Review, Hunger Mountain, Santa Fe Writers Project, Immigrant Report, Passengers Journal* and others. She is currently a PhD researcher at the University of Birmingham, England. She is the founder of www.wanderlust-Journal.com, publishing travel stories and photos from across the world. She is Editor-in-Chief at www.genderqueerliterature.org.

Sleam's 12th book, *Hidden*, was published by Finishing Line Press in 2021.

www.ingramcontent.com/pod-product-compliance
Lightning Source LLC
Chambersburg PA
CBHW031023260626
47153CB00018B/2882